THE CAT IN THE HAT

By Dr. Seuss

戴帽子的貓

文·圖　蘇斯博士
譯　詹宏志

戴帽子的貓   蘇斯博士小孩學讀書全集1

發行／1992年12月25日 初版 1 刷   2004年1月5日 新版 1 刷
著／蘇斯博士
譯／詹宏志
責任編輯／郝廣才　張玲玲　劉思源
美術編輯／李純真　郭倖惠　陳素芳
發行人／王榮文　　出版發行／遠流出版事業股份有限公司　　台北市南昌路二段 81 號 6 樓
行政院新聞局局版臺業字第 1295 號　　郵撥／0189456-1　　電話／(02)2392-6899　　傳真／(02)2392-6658
著作權顧問／蕭雄淋律師　法律顧問／王秀哲律師・董安丹律師
印製／鴻柏印刷事業股份有限公司
YL*ib* 遠流博識網 http://www.ylib.com　　E-mail:ylib@ylib.com

ISBN 957-32-1123-8　　　　　　　　　　　　　　　　　　　　　　　　　NT$ 99

The sun did not shine.
It was too wet to play.
So we sat in the house
All that cold, cold, wet day.

太陽不上班，
不能出去玩，
我們坐在屋子裡，
看著又溼又冷的下雨天。

I sat there with Sally.
We sat there, we two.
And I said, "How I wish
We had something to do!"
Too wet to go out
And too cold to play ball.
So we sat in the house.
We did nothing at all.

我和莎莉坐窗前，
兩個人，就我們。
「我好想好想，」我說：
「找些事情來做。」
下雨天不能出門，
太冷了不能打球，
我們呆坐屋子裡，
好玩事，都沒有。

But our fish said, "No ! No !
Make that cat go away !
Tell that Cat in the Hat
You do NOT want to play.
He should not be here.
He should not be about.
He should not be here
When your mother is out !"

我ㄨㄛˇ們ㄇㄣˊ的ㄉㄜ˙魚ㄩˊ大ㄉㄚˋ聲ㄕㄥ說ㄕㄨㄛ：
「不ㄅㄨˋ可ㄎㄜˇ以ㄧˇ！不ㄅㄨˋ可ㄎㄜˇ以ㄧˇ！
叫ㄐㄧㄠˋ那ㄋㄚˋ隻ㄓ貓ㄇㄠ快ㄎㄨㄞˋ走ㄗㄡˇ開ㄎㄞ！
告ㄍㄠˋ訴ㄙㄨˋ那ㄋㄚˋ戴ㄉㄞˋ帽ㄇㄠˋ子ㄗ˙的ㄉㄜ˙貓ㄇㄠ
你ㄋㄧˇ們ㄇㄣˊ不ㄅㄨˋ想ㄒㄧㄤˇ玩ㄨㄢˊ遊ㄧㄡˊ戲ㄒㄧˋ。
牠ㄊㄚ不ㄅㄨˋ該ㄍㄞ在ㄗㄞˋ這ㄓㄜˋ裡ㄌㄧˇ，
牠ㄊㄚ不ㄅㄨˋ該ㄍㄞ跑ㄆㄠˇ進ㄐㄧㄣˋ來ㄌㄞˊ。
牠ㄊㄚ不ㄅㄨˋ該ㄍㄞ在ㄗㄞˋ這ㄓㄜˋ裡ㄌㄧˇ，
趁ㄔㄣˋ你ㄋㄧˇ媽ㄇㄚ媽ㄇㄚ˙不ㄅㄨˋ在ㄗㄞˋ。」

"Now ! Now ! Have no fear.
Have no fear ! "said the cat.
"My tricks are not bad,"
Said the Cat in the Hat.
"Why, we can have
Lots of good fun, if you wish,
With a game that I call
Up-up-up with a fish !"

「哪！哪！不要怕！」
貓說：「不要怕！」
「我的把戲並不壞，」
戴帽子的貓賣個乖：
「一起玩最有趣，
試試看就知道，
這種遊戲叫做
一條魚舉得高！」

"Put me down ! " said the fish.
"This is no fun at all !
Put me down ! " said the fish.
"I do NOT wish to fall ! "

魚大叫：「放我下來！」

「這一點也不好玩！」

「放下我！」魚又說：

「我可不想跌下來！」

"Have no fear ! "said the cat.
"I will not let you fall.
I will hold you up high
As I stand on a ball.
With a book on one hand !
And a cup on my hat !
But that is not ALL I can do ! "
Said the cat...

貓說：「不要怕！
我不會讓你摔下。
我會把你舉得高，
站在球上面也不跌倒。
拿一本書在手上，
頂個杯子在頭上，
我的把戲還很多！」
貓一面表演一面說……

So all we could do was to
Sit !

    Sit !

        Sit !

           Sit !

And we did not like it.
Not one little bit.

我們只能坐窗前，
坐！

    坐！

        坐！

           坐！

我們可不喜歡，
一點也不好玩。

And then
Something went BUMP!
How that bump made us jump!

突_{ㄊㄨ}然_{ㄖㄢ}間_{ㄐㄧㄢ}，
好_{ㄏㄠ}大_{ㄉㄚ}一一聲_{ㄕㄥ} "碰_{ㄆㄥ}" ！
碰_{ㄆㄥ}一一聲_{ㄕㄥ}，嚇_{ㄒㄧㄚ}一一跳_{ㄊㄧㄠ}！

We looked !
Then we saw him step
in on the mat !
We looked !
And we saw him !
The Cat in the Hat !
And he said to us,
"Why do you sit
there like that ? "

轉頭看，
看到牠的腳跨進門！
我們看，
看到牠全身！
戴帽子的貓！
一進門，牠就說：
「你們怎麼
那樣呆呆坐？」

"I know it is wet
And the sun is not sunny.
But we can have
Lots of good fun that is funny！"

「 我知道， 天下雨，
我知道， 太陽不出來，
但是我們還有
好多好玩的事可以做！」

"I know some good games we could play,"
Said the cat.
"I know some new tricks,"
Said the Cat in the Hat.
"A lot of good tricks.
I will show them to you.
Your mother
Will not mind at all if I do."

這隻怪貓說：
「我知道一些好玩的遊戲，
我還會一些新鮮的玩意。」
戴帽子的貓又說：
「一大堆好玩的把戲，
我一樣一樣教給你，
你媽媽一定說沒關係。」

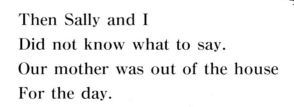

Then Sally and I
Did not know what to say.
Our mother was out of the house
For the day.

莎莉和我，
不知道該說什麼，
媽媽不在家，
教我怎麼回答牠？

"Look at me !
Look at me now !" said the cat.
"With a cup and a cake
On the top of my hat !
I can hold up TWO books !
I can hold up the fish !
And a little toy ship !
And some milk on a dish !
And look !
I can hop up and down on the ball !
But that is not all !
Oh, no.
That is not all...

「 看著我，」
貓又說：「看清楚，
一個杯子和一塊蛋糕，
在我帽子上跳舞！
手上還拿兩本書，
這隻魚不會掉下來！
看我再加一艘玩具船！
看我再加一碟鮮牛奶！
快看快看！
我還可以在球上面跳跳跳！
我的把戲還沒玩完！
當然，當然，
還沒完…… 」

"Look at me !
Look at me !
Look at me NOW !
It is fun to have fun
But you have to know how.
I can hold up the cup
And the milk and the cake !
I can hold up these books !
And the fish on a rake !
I can hold the toy ship
And a little toy man !
And look ! With my tail
I can hold a red fan !
I can fan with the fan
As I hop on the ball !
But that is not all.
Oh, no.
That is not all..."

「趕快看！
趕快看！
仔細看！
妙把戲最好玩，
你得要學得巧。
看我頂著茶杯，
拿著牛奶和蛋糕，
三本書再排一隊！
大草耙把魚缸頂上天！
玩具船停在我指尖！
再加一名玩具兵！
看，　尾巴一捲，
又是一把小紅扇，
可以給我搧搧風！
我還在球上面跳跳跳！
我的把戲還沒玩完！
當然，　當然，
還沒完……」

That is what the cat said…
Then he fell on his head !
He came down with a bump
From up there on the ball.
And Sally and I,
We saw ALL the things fall !

那隻貓正在吹大牛，
哎呀摔了個大跟頭，
好大一聲 " 碰 " ！
跌了貓， 滾了球。
我和莎莉睜大眼，
所有的東西摔得一個不留！

And our fish came down, too.
He fell into a pot !
He said, "Do I like this ?
Oh, no ! I do not.
This is not a good game,"
Said our fish as he lit.
"No, I do not like it,
Not one little bit ! "

我們的魚也摔下來，
跌到一隻茶壺裡！
魚大叫：「我怎麼會喜歡這種遊戲？
決不！決不！
這不是好玩的遊戲！」
魚從茶壺探出頭來，說：
「不，我一點也不喜歡，
你的無聊把戲！」

"Now look what you did !"
Said the fish to the cat.
"Now look at this house !
Look at this ! Look at that !
You sank our toy ship,
Sank it deep in the cake.

You shook up our house
And you bent our new rake.
You SHOULD NOT be here
When our mother is not.
You get out of this house ! "
Said the fish in the pot.

魚ㄩˊ對ㄉㄨㄟˋ貓ㄇㄠ 大ㄉㄚˋ聲ㄕㄥ 說ㄕㄨㄛ：
「 看ㄎㄢˋ看ㄎㄢˋ你ㄋㄧˇ， 做ㄗㄨㄛˋ的ㄉㄜ 好ㄏㄠˇ事ㄕˋ！
看ㄎㄢˋ看ㄎㄢˋ這ㄓㄜˋ屋ㄨ 子ㄗˇ！
你ㄋㄧˇ看ㄎㄢˋ這ㄓㄜˋ裡ㄌㄧˇ！ 你ㄋㄧˇ看ㄎㄢˋ那ㄋㄚˋ裡ㄌㄧˇ！
玩ㄨㄢˊ具ㄐㄩˋ船ㄔㄨㄢˊ沈ㄔㄣˊ沒ㄇㄟˊ了ㄌㄜ，
沈ㄔㄣˊ到ㄉㄠˋ蛋ㄉㄢˋ糕ㄍㄠ 裡ㄌㄧˇ。
屋ㄨ 子ㄗˇ裡ㄌㄧˇ搞ㄍㄠˇ亂ㄌㄨㄢˋ了ㄌㄜ，
大ㄉㄚˋ草ㄘㄠˇ耙ㄆㄚˊ也ㄧㄝˇ弄ㄋㄨㄥˋ彎ㄨㄢ 了ㄌㄜ。
媽ㄇㄚ 媽ㄇㄚ 出ㄔㄨ 門ㄇㄣˊ不ㄅㄨˊ在ㄗㄞˋ家ㄐㄧㄚ，
你ㄋㄧˇ不ㄅㄨˊ該ㄍㄞ 來ㄌㄞˊ這ㄓㄜˋ裡ㄌㄧˇ，
你ㄋㄧˇ應ㄧㄥ 該ㄍㄞ 快ㄎㄨㄞˋ離ㄌㄧˊ開ㄎㄞ ！」
說ㄕㄨㄛ話ㄏㄨㄚˋ的ㄉㄜ 魚ㄩˊ在ㄗㄞˋ茶ㄔㄚˊ壺ㄏㄨˊ裡ㄌㄧˇ。

"But I like to be here.
Oh, I like it a lot！"
Said the Cat in the Hat
To the fish in the pot.
"I will NOT go away.
I do NOT wish to go！
And so,"said the Cat in the Hat,
"So

    so

       so…

I will show you
Another good game that I know！"

戴帽子的貓
對茶壺裡的魚說：
「可是我偏要
在這裡！
我偏偏不要走，
我根本不想走！」
戴帽子的貓說：「所以啊，
所以，

    所以，

       所以……

我再來給你們
表演一個新把戲！」

And then he ran out.
And, then, fast as a fox,
The Cat in the Hat
Came back in with a box.

說完話，　他跑開，
像隻狐狸快又快，
戴帽子的貓跑回來，
一個大木箱肩上抬。

A big red wood box.
It was shut with a hook.
"Now look at this trick,"
Said the cat.
"Take a look！"

一一個紅色的大木箱，
鉤子扣著箱子的蓋。
「新把戲，要上場，」
這隻貓，又賣乖：
「快看快看，來來來！」

Then he got up on top
With a tip of his hat.
"I call this game FUN-IN-A-BOX,"
Said the cat.
"In this box are two things
I will show to you now.
You will like these two things,"
Said the cat with a bow.

爬到箱子上，
脫帽行個禮，
怪貓說：「這個遊戲
叫做妙妙箱真神奇。」
「 箱子裡有兩個妙東西，
我讓你們看仔細，
你們一定喜歡這些東西。」
說完鞠躬笑嘻嘻。

"I will pick up the hook.
You will see something new.
Two things. And I call them
Thing One and Thing Two.
These Things will not bite you.
They want to have fun."

Then, out of the box
Came Thing Two and Thing One !
And they ran to us fast.
They said,"How do you do ?
Would you like to shake hands
With Thing One and Thing Two ?"

「 我把鉤子輕輕拉起，
你們就看到新鮮東西。
這兩個玩意，我叫他們
一個是東西甲，
一個是東西乙。
兩個東西不咬人，
只是喜歡玩遊戲。」

說完話，箱子裡
跑出了東西甲
和東西乙！
他們快跑到面前，
同聲說：「你們好！
要不要握個手？
我是東西甲，
他是東西乙！」

And Sally and I
Did not know what to do.
So we had to shake hands
With Thing One and Thing Two.
We shook their two hands.
But our fish said, "No！No！
Those Things should not be
In this house！Make them go！

我和莎莉
覺得很有趣，
我們伸出手，
和東西甲，　也和東西乙，
拉拉手行個禮。
但我們的魚說：「不可以，　不可以！
這兩個東西不該在屋子裡，
叫他們快出去！」

"They should not be here
When your mother is not !
Put them out ! Put them out !"
Said the fish in the pot.

「 媽媽出門不在，
他們不該來這裡，
叫他們快離開！ 叫他們快離開！」
生氣的魚在茶壺裡。

"Have no fear, little fish,"
Said the Cat in the Hat.
"These Things are good Things."
And he gave them a pat.
"They are tame. Oh, so tame!
They have come here to play.
They will give you some fun
On this wet, wet, wet day."

「不要怕，小乖魚，」
怪貓說話變得輕聲細氣：
「這些東西不是壞東西。」
怪貓伸手摸摸他們的頭。
「他們很乖，真的很乖！
他們只是來玩一玩，
你們一定會很喜歡，
在這種又溼又冷的下雨天。」

"Now, here is a game that they like,"
Said the cat.
"They like to fly kites,"
Said the Cat in the Hat.

「看ㄎㄢˋ，　這ㄓㄜˋ種ㄓㄨㄥˇ遊ㄧㄡˊ戲ㄒㄧˋ他ㄊㄚ們ㄇㄣ最ㄗㄨㄟˋ愛ㄞˋ。」
貓ㄇㄠ閉ㄅㄧˋ著ㄓㄜ眼ㄧㄢˇ睛ㄐㄧㄥ説ㄕㄨㄛ。
「看ㄎㄢˋ，　放ㄈㄤˋ風ㄈㄥ箏ㄓㄥ眞ㄓㄣ不ㄅㄨˋ賴ㄌㄞˋ。」
我ㄨㄛˇ們ㄇㄣ睜ㄓㄥ大ㄉㄚˋ眼ㄧㄢˇ睛ㄐㄧㄥ看ㄎㄢˋ。

"No ! Not in the house !"
Said the fish in the pot.
"They should not fly kites
In a house ! They should not.
Oh, the things they will bump !
Oh, the things they will hit !
Oh, I do not like it !
Not one little bit !"

「不可以！ 在屋子裡不可以！」
茶壺裡的魚很生氣。
「不可以在屋子裡
放風箏， 絕對不可以！
啊， 他們會碰上東西！
啊， 他們會撞壞東西！
我絕對不容許， 千萬不可以！」

Then Sally and I
Saw them run down the hall.
We saw those two Things
Bump their kites on the wall !
Bump ! Thump ! Thump ! Bump !
Down the wall in the hall.

於是我和莎莉
看著他們跑到大廳裡。
那兩個寶貝東西
把風箏撞上了牆壁！
乒乒乒乒！ 乒乒乒乒！
好像倒了牆翻了地！

Thing Two and Thing One!
They ran up! They ran down!
On the string of one kite
We saw Mother's new gown!
Her gown with the dots
That are pink, white and red.
Then we saw one kite bump
On the head of her bed!

東西甲和東西乙，
他們跑東又跑西！
一個風箏的線，
勾住了媽媽的新衣！
這件衣服媽媽最中意，
粉紅、大紅的
圓點配上白底。
然後我們又看見
另一個風箏刮到了
媽媽的床邊。

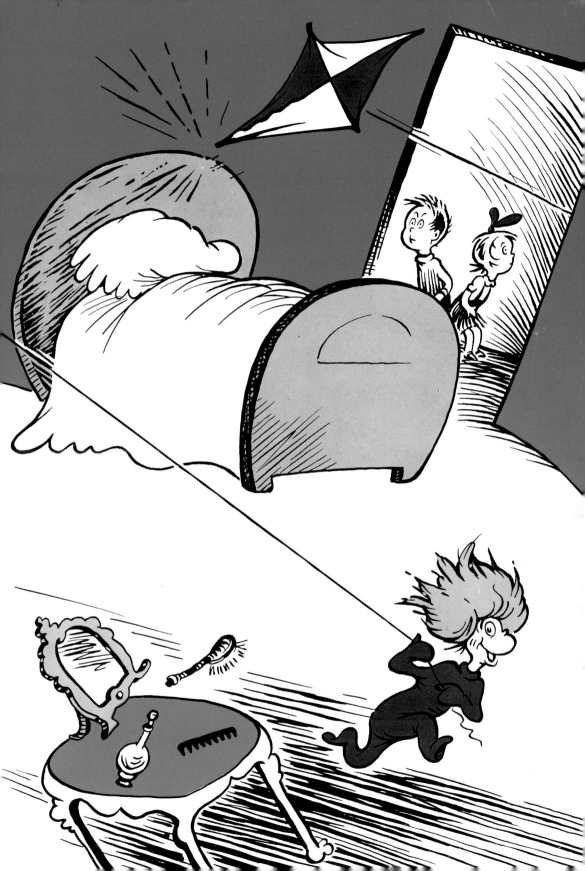

Then those Things ran about
With big bumps, jumps and kicks
And with hops and big thumps
And all kinds of bad tricks.
And I said,
"I do NOT like the way
that they play !
If Mother could see this,
Oh, what would she say !"

兩個東西到處亂跑，
又撞，　又踢，　又跳！
大聲吵還用力敲，
各種壞樣子都
使盡了。
我就說話了：
「　我不喜歡他們
這樣玩遊戲，
媽媽要是看到了，
一定會生氣！」

Then our fish said, "Look ! Look !"
And our fish shook with fear.
"Your mother is on her way home !
Do you hear ?
Oh, what will she do to us ?
What will she say ?
Oh, she will not like it
To find us this way !"

我們的魚突然叫起來：
「快看！ 快看！」一面說一面發抖。
「你媽媽回來了！
你們聽到了沒有？
啊， 她會怎麼說？
她會對我們做什麼？
啊， 她一定不喜歡
看到房子裡七零八落！」

"So, DO something ! Fast !" said the fish.
"Do you hear !
I saw her. Your mother !
Your mother is near !
So, as fast as you can,
Think of something to do !
You will have to get rid of
Thing One and Thing Two !"

魚說：「趕快！ 想點辦法！
聽到了嗎？
我看到了你媽媽，
她已經快到家！
聽到了沒有？
趕快趕快，
想想辦法，
想辦法弄走這個
東西乙和東西甲！」

So, as fast as I could,
I went after my net.
And I said, "With my net
I can get them I bet.
I bet, with my net,
I can get those Things yet !"

說多快有多快，
快拿我的網子來。
我說：「拿我的網子來，
我就可以把他們抓起來。
看我的厲害，
我一次就把兩個抓起來。」

Then I let down my net.
It came down with a PLOP!
And I had them! At last!
Those two Things had to stop.
Then I said to the cat,
"Now you do as I say.
You pack up those Things.
And you take them away!"

撲下我的網，
"啪啦" 一聲響！
兩個東西逃不掉，
終於被我抓到了。
我就對貓說：
「現在要趕快，
收拾這兩個東西，
把他們帶離開！」

"Oh dear !" said the cat.
"You did not like our game...
Oh dear.
What a shame !
What a shame !
What a shame !"

「天啊！」怪貓嘆口氣，
「你們都不喜歡我的遊戲，
天啊！ 實在太可惜！
太可惜！
太可惜！」

Then he shut up the Things
In the box with the hook.
And the cat went away
With a sad kind of look.

他_{ㄊㄚ}收_{ㄕㄡ}拾_ㄕ了_{ㄌㄜ}東_{ㄉㄨㄥ}西_{ㄒㄧ}，
放_{ㄈㄤ}進_{ㄐㄧㄣ}箱_{ㄒㄧㄤ}子_ㄗ扣_{ㄎㄡ}上_{ㄕㄤ}鉤_{ㄍㄡ}，
抬_{ㄊㄞ}著_{ㄓㄜ}走_{ㄗㄡ}出_{ㄔㄨ}去_{ㄑㄩ}，
神_{ㄕㄣ}情_{ㄑㄧㄥ}很_{ㄏㄣ}憂_{ㄧㄡ}愁_{ㄔㄡ}。

"That is good," said the fish.
"He has gone away. Yes.
But your mother will come.
She will find this big mess !
And this mess is so big
And so deep and so tall,
We can not pick it up.
There is no way at all !"

魚說：「牠走了，
這就好。
你媽媽也快來到，
她會看到這些亂七八糟。
東西堆得這麼多，
這麼亂，真糟糕，
我們根本收不了，
怎麼辦才好？」

And THEN !
Who was back in the house ?
Why, the cat !
"Have no fear of this mess,"
Said the Cat in the Hat.
"I always pick up all my playthings
And so...
I will show you another
Good trick that I know!"

突然間，
誰又來到房子裡面？
是貓！ 我的天！
「 不要擔心不要怕！」
戴帽子的貓說大話：
「 玩過的東西要收好，
看看我……
你們就知道，
我也是個好寶寶！」

Then we saw him pick up
All the things that were down.
He picked up the cake,
And the rake, and the gown,
And the milk, and the strings,
And the books, and the dish,
And the fan, and the cup,
And the ship, and the fish.
And he put them away.
Then he said, "That is that."
And then he was gone
With a tip of his hat.

我們看牠開怪車，
七手八腳收東西。
蛋糕撿起來，
草耙收起來，
還有媽媽的新衣，
風箏收起來，
擦擦牛奶灑的地，
書本撿起來，
碟子放到櫥子裡。
還有扇子，　還有杯子，
還有船，　還有生氣的魚。
貓說：「這就好。」
脫帽行個禮，
車子開走不見了。

Then our mother came in
And she said to us two,
"Did you have any fun?
Tell me. What did you do?"
And Sally and I did not know
What to say.
Should we tell her
The things that went on there that day?

媽媽走進門，
開口問我們：
「你們在家玩什麼？
做什麼？ 告訴我。」
我和莎莉， 我看你，
你看我，
不知道該說什麼。
今天的怪事怎麼說？

Should we tell her about it?
Now, what SHOULD we do?
Well…
What would YOU do
If your mother asked YOU?

該　不　該　跟　媽　媽　說？
要　怎　麼　說？
嗯……
告　訴　我，　如　果　是　你
媽　媽　問　起，　你　怎　麼　說？